P9-BZJ-765

WELCOME TO
PASSPORT TO READING
A beginning reader's ticket to a brand-new world!

Every book in this program is designed to build read-along and read-alone skills, level by level, through engaging and enriching stories. As the reader turns each page, he or she will become more confident with new vocabulary, sight words, and comprehension.

These PASSPORT TO READING levels will help you choose the perfect book for every reader.

READING TOGETHER
Read short words in simple sentence structures together to begin a reader's journey.

READING OUT LOUD
Encourage developing readers to sound out words in more complex stories with simple vocabulary.

READING INDEPENDENTLY
Newly independent readers gain confidence reading more complex sentences with higher word counts.

READY TO READ MORE
Readers prepare for chapter books with fewer illustrations and longer paragraphs.

This book features sight words from the educator-supported Dolch Sight Word List. Readers will become more familiar with these commonly used vocabulary words, increasing reading speed and fluency.

For more information, please visit www.passporttoreadingbooks.com.

Enjoy the journey!

Copyright © 2003 by Todd Parr

All rights reserved. In accordance with the U.S. Copyright Act of 1976, the scanning, uploading, and electronic sharing of any part of this book without the permission of the publisher is unlawful piracy and theft of the author's intellectual property. If you would like to use material from the book (other than for review purposes), prior written permission must be obtained by contacting the publisher at permissions@hbgusa.com. Thank you for your support of the author's rights.

Little, Brown and Company

Hachette Book Group
237 Park Avenue, New York, NY 10017
Visit our website at www.lb-kids.com

Little, Brown and Company is a division of Hachette Book Group, Inc.
The Little, Brown name and logo are trademarks of Hachette Book Group, Inc.

The publisher is not responsible for websites (or their content)
that are not owned by the publisher.

First Revised Edition: May 2014
Adapted from *Otto Goes to the Beach*,
first published in hardcover in May 2003 by Little, Brown and Company

Library of Congress Cataloging-in-Publication Data

Parr, Todd.
Otto goes to the beach / Todd Parr. — 1st ed.
p. cm.
Summary: When Otto the dog feels lonely, he drives to the beach hoping to find
a friend to play with.
ISBN 978-0-316-73870-5 (hc)—ISBN 978-0-316-24602-6 (pb)
[1. Dogs—Fiction. 2. Friendship—Fiction. 3. Beaches—Fiction. 4. Animals—Fiction.] I. Title.
PZ7.P2447 Ot 2003
[E]—dc21

2002072986

10 9 8 7 6 5 4 3 2 1

SC

Printed in China

Passport to Reading titles are leveled by independent reviewers applying the standards developed by
Irene Fountas and Gay Su Pinnell in *Matching Books to Readers: Using Leveled Books in
Guided Reading*, Heinemann, 1999.

OTTO
Goes to the Beach

TODD PARR

L B
LITTLE, BROWN AND COMPANY
New York   Boston

This is Otto.

"Woof, woof!" he says.

Otto is home by himself.
He is sad.
He wants to play
with someone.

Poor Otto!

Otto needs to find a friend.
He drives to the beach.

Otto sits in his beach chair.
He puts on sunscreen.
He looks for a friend.

Otto sees a crab.
"Do you want
to make a sand castle?"
he asks.
"No," says the crab.
"I am too crabby!"

Poor Otto!

Otto meets some fish.
He tries to swim with them.
They swim the other way.

Poor Otto!

Otto is hungry.
He goes to the snack bar.
Otto asks for a bone.
The snack bar has
only ice cream.

Poor Otto!

Otto buys some ice cream.
It melts all over his nose.

Poor Otto!

Otto meets a cat.
Otto and the cat go surfing.
"This is fun!" says Otto.

A big wave splashes over them.
It makes Otto's bathing suit
fall down.
The cat laughs at Otto.

Poor Otto!

Otto is sad.
Will he ever find a friend?
He decides to take a nap.

Otto wakes up
when he hears a dog.
"Bark, bark!" says the dog.
Her name is Noodle Poodle.

"Do you want to play with me?"
Noodle Poodle asks.
She is digging up bones.
"Yes," says Otto.
"I love to dig."

Otto and Noodle Poodle play
in the water all day long.
Otto is not lonely.
He has a new friend.

LUCKY OTTO!

A note from Todd:

Sometimes it is hard
to make new friends.
Remember, there is
always someone
out there to
play with you!

LOVE, ♡

OTTO and Todd